The Look Away

XYOI

THE

LOOK AWAY

Richard Skelton

XYLEM BOOKS

2018

XY01 The Look Away (2018)

The Look Away

Copyright © Richard Skelton 2018
The author's moral rights have been asserted

First published in 2018 by Corbel Stone Press
This edition copyright © Xylem Books 2018

ISBN: 978-1-9999718-0-9

Xylem Books is an imprint of Corbel Stone Press

I

I am north of where I was. Go north. That was the imperative. Always north. Although the why of it is no longer clear. Follow the needle. He leadeth me in the paths.

+

The old prayers, unsaid for decades, come back unbidden. Ghosts. Empty conjurings. Dry on the tongue.

+

In a rocky hollow you will find an old shieling. I'll lay me here a while. Safe in the middle of hills. Surely.

You didn't give her your name, did you? Here's
all I have, I said, giving her the money. The sum
total of a life. Are you come here to die? she said,
like she meant it. I don't remember. Leave a list
in this bag and hang it by the field-gate, once a
week. You'll get you what you need. She seemed
to understand it better than I did myself. Done
this before? I asked. She didn't reply.

+

Near darkness. A steep climb. A field-gate.
A rough track through the field, still climbing.
And then a low stone hut. Thickset walls.
Built, surely, to keep out something other than
weather. Goodness and mercy. You could bury
a body in there. Lengthways.

+

Are you come here to die? She must have seen the blood. I tried to walk straight but her eyes said it. You look in bad shape, boy.

+

And now I drift in and out. In and out. This cannot be good. I gave her all the money. The sum total. Who is that, there? My heart. Hello?

+

There is nothing for it. I'll lay me here. Nothing to be done. How to fill the black hours? Voices. At the threshold of hearing. Flashlights? I cannot tell.

+

Three cramped rooms and no running water.
A well in the yard. No toilet but a stone
outhouse. A hearth but no heat. Even if there
was wood to burn I will not risk a fire. I will
not give a sign to be found. I will be ready.

+

You didn't give her your name, did you? Be still.
The pain is unbearable at times. To move is
agony.

+

Each day the rain, ceaseless. The sound like nothing I can tell.

+

What made people climb up into these hills, centuries ago? To a place where even water does not stay, but runs, as fast as it can, to lower ground? What had they done, that they would hide up here? Is it safe?

+

Bed down there. Out of sight. Prepare yourself. They will come. Think on that.

+

Some bearings. Whitewashed walls. Clean enough, but there is mould in the air. In the largest room a wooden table. A chair. A chest, empty, except for some blankets and a handful of candles. A washstand and basin. A large horseshoe nailed to one of the roof-beams. On the wall a pendulum clock, still ticking. A large map over the mantlepiece. Near the door a small cold-room. In the other room a narrow bed. A bed-stand. Another smaller horseshoe. Only one door to the front of the building. Windows the only other means of escape. When my strength returns I will move the bed into the corner of the main room. I will face the door even in sleep.

+

Who is that? Who is there? I know there is someone but I do not see you.

+

I will not give a sign. Touch the horseshoes. Cross yourself. Say His name if you think it will help. He leadeth me in the paths. I will dwell in the house—

+

I remember almost nothing of the journey.
A flight in the dark and I was only half-
conscious. Hovering on a threshold. Sluggish
with analgesics. The pain receding to a dull ache.
Lulled by the motion of the car. Its low engine
murmur. The blur of passing headlights.
How did I drive the thing so bloody?

+

I can still hear the strain of the engine climbing
those last miles. Can feel the sting of the cold,
damp air as I stowed the car in the wood. Out
of sight.

+

Goodness and mercy. I try to remember more but it escapes me. Perhaps I have a fever. Am I where I should be? Go north. He leadeth me in the paths. To the limits of the map. The nameless country. The empty page. You didn't give her your name, did you?

+

Bread, butter and cheese. A jar of bitter damson jam and some slices of cured ham wrapped in waxed paper. In the little time that I have been here, these things have become the centre of my world. I arrange them on the shelves of the cold-room obsessively. It has the look of a shrine. Meagre offerings to a departed god.

+

All impossibly tangled. I see everything but what I want to see. Disconnected images. Havoc. Disorder. Something has broken loose. Up there. I shudder at the thought.

+

The interior of the car. Moving at great speed.
In the windshield a bright, indistinct blur, lit by
headlights in the night's darkness. Taking on
form. You didn't, did you?

+

A figure, arms outstretched, waving pathetically,
mouth opening and closing, undoubtedly
emitting a panicked cry, unheard, drowned
out by traffic. You didn't?

+

And then gone. Swallowed by the distance.
Down the road's long, dark throat.

Each time, in the dead of night, I awaken. Dry mouth. Chest tight. Struggling for breath. The pain flaring. That contorted afterimage filling the room as my hands flail. Feeling for light.

But there are no lights here. Nothing except an intermittent, white glow at the periphery of my vision. Swirling patterns of blue and green. Pinpoints of red. It is as if my eyes are filling in for the darkness, which is not merely a lack of light, but its utter negation.

And so I sit the whole night through. Hunched in the corner. Back against the wall. The pain and the dark show.

+

You look in bad shape, boy. Bed down there.
Rest a while. You'll get used to it. You could bury
a body in there. Whitewashed walls. The sum
total of a life.

+

I see fields and meadows. An old, winding country lane. Low hills hazed in the distance. A family, walking. The boy trails slightly behind the others.

At a bend in the lane his eye is caught by something in the hedgerow. A bird's nest, with the mother crouched down, brooding. She returns his gaze, sidelong, unblinking. Her large, dark eye bright with fear. Just one, the boy sings to her, gently, just this once.

Meagre, grey dawns. Rain after rain. I haven't left the shieling in a week. Not that I would. I will lie low. Swirling patterns. Bread and butter. My cup runneth—

+

The pain subsides if I lie perfectly still. But even then I feel movement. Not the dull workings of my own body, but something greater. It is another body, massive and restless, shifting beneath me. Rising and falling. My mind drifts, and although I cannot hear it, I feel the progress of the stream that runs close by. Its thousand veins meeting other tracts of water, seen and unseen. The hills' open pores, fractures and fault lines, flooded with dark liquid. And so my body, filled with blood, water, mucus.

+

Do not stray too far. Stay close to the edge. The waters run deep.

+

I try the windows but they will not move.
Probably swollen shut for years. Caked in mould.
This place begins to feel like a cage. Or a trap.

+

The rain ceased a few days ago, only to be replaced by mist. I miss the sound of it. More than that, I long for the din of humanity, machinery, life. A soft bed of noise on which to rest the ears. Anything but this hard silence. This unnatural quiet. I hear only the muted ticking of the clock and the muffled, uneven workings of my own body. Both plague me with their insistence.

+

The pain seems to increase, not diminish. I dress and undress the wound obsessively.

+

Blood, water, mucus. Something has broken loose. Taking on form. I know it.

+

I day-dream of analgesia. A child's sleep. A rest that is the gift of innocence.

+

The butter is gone and this black bread sticks to the teeth. I count the days until fresh provisions will arrive. I've followed her instructions to the letter, but my requests are often ignored. *You'll get you what you need.* Fruit, chocolate, alcohol. After only a few weeks these things seem like fables.

+

Perpetual mist. Occasional glimpse of field or hill. No sounds. Everything muted. The world turned to grey. But surely I should take comfort from the fact that I am now doubly hidden. First, by the folds of these sodden hills, which seem to tighten in around me, and second, by this near-impenetrable grey-white cloak. I am an island lost in an infinite sea.

+

Another evening falls. No lights except those in my head. And the images that come from the dark. I comfort myself with the thought that they are simply a delusion. Sometimes I think I see a figure. A darker shadow in the corner of the room. Who there? Show yourself. What do you want?

+

Are you come here to die? A wordless question. An insinuation of the damp air. Touch the horseshoes. Goodness and mercy.

+

The mist has partially retreated and I venture outside. I see a glacier-ravaged terrain. A narrow valley. The nameless country.

Near-vertical scree-slopes. Banks of burnt-looking bracken. Small isolated trees, bent double from exposure in postures of apparent distress. The rough track that winds its way up from the field-gate, although clearly well-worn from centuries of use, is overgrown and untended. The fields themselves are empty, except for the sunken forms of derelict machinery.

The men have gone, abandoning their instruments. The regalia of deposed kings. And I am their successor. Heir to a land returned to nature.

+

The compass sits on the window ledge, its needle pointing up the hollow road. Go north, it urges. Another day, perhaps. But today I can barely stand.

+

You didn't give her your name, did you? My name is nothing here. There is no one. I sink into anonymity. Friendships, enmities, all gone. I cannot conjure even one of them. I am lost. Who there?

+

More bearings. The shieling is hemmed-in by various outbuildings, all in various stages of dereliction. The nearest, a low, narrow byre, broods darkness. Shaded by an ash-tree, its doorway—the door itself having long rotted away—grants only scant light to within. Even on the brightest day. Earlier this morning I crossed the threshold, fringed with nettles, only to stumble back, moments later, stinging my ankles, cursing. I returned with a broom salvaged from one of the other buildings and beat back the weeds with a savagery that frightened me.

And my violence disturbed something. A small pale bird, clearly much distressed, rose up in front of me, hovering frantically in the middle of the room, turning ever tighter circles in the air in its vaulting panic. It uttered not a sound but I could hear the beating of its wings, seemingly from all corners of the room. And beneath it the thing to which it seemed tethered. A large, rusted sculpture of twisted wire.

In those brief, half-lit moments it felt as if I was at the centre of an awful gyre, that I was party to a premonition of purgatory. The panic was contagious and I turned to leave. Not looking back.

+

The nettle rash has long disappeared but those moments still itch like a newly formed scar. And now I find myself looking in the direction of that narrow storehouse, its tin roof tacked over a crumbling shell, protecting an already weather-worn coil of metal. Why enshrine something already sacrificed to rust?

I try to recall my impression of the wire structure itself. My memory of those moments is distorted and each time the thing takes on a different form. It is as if my mind, doubting the memory, is conjuring it afresh. A sprawling lattice. A contorted human shape. An elaborate snare. A twisted crown.

And more and more my mind is drawn to the bird that dwells in the dark. I can still hear the beating of its wings. What fate binds it to this place, to that byre, and to that rusted coil?

+

A feeling of nausea overwhelms me. Everywhere I go, there is damage. Go north. There is nothing for you here.

+

I gave her all. The sum total. There is no one.
I'll lay me here. I am lost.

+

The map hanging over the mantlepiece is a
singular piece of work. The south-east corner is
finely drawn up to the banks of a river that I will
not name. Clearly some kind of boundary, but
beyond that I cannot say. It feels like the edge of
an abyss. The rest of the map is a wasteland of
white. An empty quarter. Go north. I remember
now. To the limits of the map. Out of sight.
I am here.

+

I notice that some of the place-names penned
into the corner of the map are those of animals:
hare, fox, raven. And there among them, circled
heavily in pencil, I see the name carved in the
lintel above the door of this very dwelling,
Hollowscar, with the word *ruins* in brackets
beneath it.

I see now that there are other pencil lines. Arcs
and circles—faint but measured and precise. Not
contours, but something else. A sprawling lattice.
Emanating from the shieling and taking in the
whole hollow. Bisecting the names of things.
Bringing them together. I step back, trying
to make sense of it all. The date reads 20th of
December, 1850.

+

Beyond the shieling, the hills loom, lean in, suffocate. The sun is mostly absent. On those rare clear days, no sooner has it risen above one hill ridge than it seems to have already slipped beyond the other, describing a low, shallow arc in the sky. The shadow of that hill—the one that rises steeply up behind the shieling—then creeps across the field to its front, and begins its ascent of the facing slope. It reminds me of a stalking animal. At such times it feels as though the hills will collapse inwardly, and there is a warm afterglow of sunset, like a dim candle in a far-off room. If enough time were to pass I am sure these hills will eventually heal over that great wound caused by ice, millennia ago. I am strangely comforted by such thoughts.

+

Hollowscar. The name is like a threat. What am I doing here? How long has it been? I cannot tell.

✝

The old ash-tree that shades the byre. When the wind picks up I hear the drag of its knuckles across the battered tin roof. It is almost a caress. When I think of it, rooted there for centuries, I think of madness.

But hare, fox, and raven are rooted too. Written *down*. Mapped. Who would pin the names of those wild, free things to this or that field, stream or hill? Surely that is madness? And in the havoc of my mind I know that even trees once roamed free.

+

I have not see the boy in a long time. Am I losing everything? No. There are others. You'll get you what you need. I can still hear the beating of its wings.

+

What lies in the empty quarter? According
to the map, this small valley runs almost
perpendicular to a ridge of hills whose north-
western slopes descend into the abyssal river.
I fantasise about following the hollow road as
it climbs to the valley rim, so that I might look
out over the map's white void, across the vast
expanse of nothingness.

+

Are you come here to die? Nothingness is my
answer.

+

Perhaps my ears are becoming attuned to the life that lives below silence. The stream that runs close by. At night I hear it more and more. Running, running. Its dark motion like a chant.

+

Courage. When dusk is in full bloom I sometimes leave the shieling to walk the rough track that winds through the field below. I walk slowly and never far, keeping the shieling within view. I often find myself looking back for reassurance. Each step made away is an unmooring. I wish I had a rope to tether myself. I feel that I might slip, lose my footing, stumble into the unknown. Despite my fragility of mind I know that this is not merely a delusion. There are things lost here. Unable to fly. I can feel it.

As I walk and darkness slowly descends, the colour gradually bleeds from the world. At some indefinable moment I know that it is only memory telling me that the fields are green. My eyes tell me they are grey. Eventually, even the greys recede into the blackness. This slow loss of sight's faculty is unsettling. So much of my past is fading. And I am losing more each day. Sometimes it grows so dark that I have to feel my way back along the trail of tumbled walls. Bats fill the air above me, moving unceasingly to-and-fro, and I hear owls calling in the woodland lower down the hollow. There are other sounds, too, which I hesitate to identify. Sounds which belong to the night.

+

And so conscience tells me that I have done something unspeakable. But in this perpetual dark I cannot see it. Cannot even touch it.

+

What lies hidden, deep in these silted backwaters, waiting to be carried downstream?

+

Something buried in the sediment. Beyond arm's reach. And it frightens me.

+

I see a farm. The boy walks out past the paddock fence strung with its gallery of dead moles. Out through the stackyard where an adder is sunning itself. Out through the fields, beyond the drystone walls, along the sheep-paths, up through the gorse and bracken.

It is lambing season and he sits beneath a rowan tree, looking down on the farm, listening to the sound of it all. The mothers crying for their young, the young crying for their mothers. The mothers and young running to-and-fro, to-and-fro, reunited, separated, reunited again. A comic opera.

When he returns for supper he sees a ewe still birthing. The lamb half hanging out of her. Sickly thin legs, impossibly long, wreathed in blood. Not moving. And the ewe is eating grass, seemingly oblivious. And the grass behind her is a dark stain.

And he runs and runs up through the fields, through the stackyard, past the mole-fence, through the paddock until he arrives at the farmhouse door, knocking, knocking, so out-of-breath he thinks he'll keel over.

And the door opens and he spills the story all over the father's shoes, who just stoops down and pats the boy's shoulder and says he'll stroll down after supper and take a look.

And he pleads with the father, trying to convey the urgency of the situation, the horror of it. And the mother and father exchange looks in unspoken understanding of this small, pitiable, loss of innocence.

And the father just keeps patting the boy on the shoulder, saying it will be alright.

Small miracle of dreamless sleep, but it lasts too briefly. I awoke at some point in the night with dead hands. The numbness was so complete that I began to fear it was irreversible. Goodness and mercy. I lay there, hands entwined across my chest, and wondered if it would spread, rather than dissipate. Stealing down my arms, across my chest, up my neck, along my jaw. Perhaps this is how death stakes its claim on the body during sleep? Had I entered that boundary land from which there is no returning? The nameless country. Follow me.

+

Go north. I'll lay me here a while. It feels a lifetime. This cannot continue. It is little better than a prison. The chanting of the waters. I can hear it. Even in daytime. And still they do not come.

+

The same now-old game with the well-pump. Each time I can feel the muscles in my back and arms. I am sure it reopens the wound, too. I can feel it. And the water so cold it burns.

+

Last night in the cold-room I found a spirit
stove. Why did she not tell me? It was hidden
on the high shelf inside a cardboard box with
something indistinct scrawled on it in pencil.
And also an empty canister of alcohol and a box
of damp, useless matches. But at least there is
now the possibility of soup, boiled vegetables—
of warmth. I have begun to feel a creeping
cold in the bones. The wound still aches and I
have no fresh dressing. Only a few pain-killers
left, which I ration and use only at night. New
items for the list: gauze, matches, ethanol, tea,
potatoes, carrots.

+

In those first weeks I spent most of my hours
huddled before the window, a kind of fear
possessing me. An awful anticipation. But
nothing came. Nothing but shadows. This is an
unregarded place. Even the wind does not linger.

+

Soap that barely lathers in cold water. An outhouse toilet that is little better than a hole in the ground. What is there to stop me walking down the hollow road and back into civilisation? They have not come. It becomes increasingly clear to me that I am forgotten.

+

Daily I fantasise about being discovered. An end to the waiting. How different to those first days here. Once I was awoken by a cacophony. My heart leapt into my throat and beat so hard I thought I would choke. It was a flock of geese flying up the hollow. But suddenly their formation dispersed, its lines broken. The sound intensified as they circled, perhaps attempting to regroup. I stumbled outside, but they were gone, their voices lost in the maw of clouds.

+

Still no reply to my last request. Yesterday I found an axe in one of the outbuildings and now it lies beneath the bed. While it is blunt, and there is no room to swing it, it reassures me. They will come. Surely. I have to believe it.

+

Violence. Havoc. It is in me, I think. There is a pit inside. A cage, a trap, in there, somewhere. I only hope it will hold.

+

I wonder if I will ever see the boy again? I feel a soft pain in my heart when he comes. I will close my eyes for him.

+

Candles but no matches. Spirit stove but no fuel. I am reduced to the life of a wild animal. I might as well drink at the stream, rather than work the wretched pump. I write and rewrite the list. It has become an invocation, or a prayer.

+

I gave her all. Near darkness. So dark. I cannot tell. Voices, on the threshold of hearing. Delusion, surely. I wish I—

+

This evening I returned from my walk early
to discover a beautiful moth on the outside
of my window. Surely drawn by some oblique
reflection of the sun's last rays. It stayed there
in perfect stillness for some time, and I studied
it intently through the glass in the fading
light. I observed the perfect arrangement of its
miniature anatomy. The colour of its camouflage
like mottled autumn leaves. One of its hind-
wings, I noticed, had sustained an injury. I felt a
pang of sympathy. We had both made a flight in
the dark. And as I looked past its frail, delicate
body to the world beyond, which seemed to fall
away around it, I felt a kind of fear.

And suddenly the moth leapt backwards into
the void of night and was gone. Such was the
intimacy with which I had observed it, that I
was stunned by its leaving. Thinking of its small
form lost within the vast dark I felt a choking,
fluttering feeling in my throat. How can such a
thing survive out there?

But later, in the dead of night, I thought this.
Wherever you are, you are free. Beyond reproach.
Even if you did not make it, you are free. You have
escaped. Nameless and beautiful.

+

The next morning, outside the shieling door, I found a neat circle of blood-stained grass with a halo of small, pale feathers. A kill. Not a bone or scrap of flesh remained. And the field glistening with dew.

Was it the bird that dwells in the dark? For some reason I will not venture back into the byre to find out. More and more it seems like a sanctum. An almery of the sacred host.

+

Have I begun to lose myself? I feel my edges begin to blur. The usual chatter of the mind recedes and thoughts come to me that are not my own.

+

—A stone, wet and shining, fresh from the waters. Black and bright at the same time. But soon enough the wetness leaves, and the glamour is gone. Give it back—

+

I wonder about the well, the stream, the water. I have rationed the food but drunk deeply and often. It seemed in no small supply—the taste like nothing I have experienced before. And I have washed in its stinging cold. Bathed the wound in it. Repeatedly.

But where has it journeyed? What tracings has it leeched from the hills' pores? What if it is tainted?

+

Sometimes I catch my own reflection in the glass. I look at the figure before me, transparent and thin, barely there, with something approaching detachment. The kind of curiosity I might have for a field, a drystone wall, a tree. Look away.

I must admit, I do not connect myself with that face, those arms and torso. Is this what it is to be human? I am adrift. At times, even words seem oddly impersonal. When I think of the word 'face' I am more likely to describe the hill that faces me. The hill that not only seems to return my gaze, but which stares right into me, through me, beyond me, as if I did not exist. Perhaps I grow as thin and insubstantial as the figure in the glass. I scream and shout. Just to hear my echo come back to me from across the hollow.

+

Day sinks into night. The pulse slackens. The wetness leaves.

+

On what passes for a clear day I sit in the window until after dusk, watching the raking sun drag its last light across the hollow. There is something in the shape of the cragged hill that faces the shieling. I am convinced of it.

Its outline, its contours, the patterning of its drystone walls, the play of shape and shadow, all suggest a form that is other than hill or mountain. And yes, sometimes when I catch it off-guard, it seems to tremble, momentarily. Like a bird. A great bird. Shaking rain off its feathers.

+

More and more, I feel the rising and falling of a great body. The pulsing of its lightless blood. Deep below the surface. I cannot deny it. My body is a single nerve, feeling, feeling.

+

—Nothing is impermeable. There are fractures, planes of weakness, wounds. There can be no resistance. The current is too strong. In the end, everything yields, surrenders, washes away—

+

Go north. Follow the needle. I am caught in the snare of these hills. Unable to fly. Am I the first, or have there been others, their minds slowly unravelling with the pain of it? Are you come here to die? she said. Her voice meant it.

+

I find now that I keep a vigil at the window from just before dusk. Can it be that the world of things is not dull, inert, unfeeling?

+

—Thou anointest my head—

+

And yes. The hills. Trembling. It is like the tensioned jaws of a trap. Surely. I have to escape.

+

I see the boy, hunting for butterflies in the wild, uncultivated land beyond the last drystone wall. As he moves he disturbs a young rabbit, lying prone beneath a matte of gorse branches. The animal's eyes are swollen shut, and there are ugly tumours along the length of its face.

It sounds like myxomatosis, says the father. Bring me to it. The kindest thing is to put it out of its misery.

Look away, the father says, if you're scared. He wrings its neck and lays it back down gently into the gorse. There, it's over now. Sleeping peacefully.

Later, over supper, the boy watches the father break bread with the same hands that broke the rabbit's neck. The same hands that lifted him over the stile when he was too small, that patted his shoulder when he was upset. A mercy killing. A death of kindness. We offer thanks to the Lord our God.

I see no more. A quickening of the river, its load increasing, taking on sediment. Dark, turbid.

Something must give. This cannot continue.
Have courage.

+

On the map, in the place where I stand, below the word *ruins*, I place my own name. A mark to go with all the others. *I was here, too.*

+

I leave the shieling before dawn and walk down
the field track, stopping at a broken line of
drystone wall that offers a good vantage from
which to watch the road without being seen.
I crouch down and make myself as comfortable
as possible.

Nothing for the longest period. Then,
somewhere far off, the repeated chanting of a
thrush, reverberating up the hollow. The sound
stands my hairs on end. Perhaps it will dispel the
pall that hangs over the valley? Above the crags to
the east I begin to see the faint blush of morning.
The song, which in the darkness seemed thin and
tentative, grows stronger, more insistent. Two
notes repeated four times, three notes five times,
a trill, a single note six times in quick succession.
Endless variations. I feel a soft, radiant pain in my
chest. A shimmering warmth that seems to leap
out of my body across the void between us. We
two strangers in the fading dark.

But the moment passes as quickly as it came,
and the bird falls abruptly silent. Was he
suddenly aware of my eavesdropping, and with
that knowledge was the spell broken?

Minutes later the answer—and the reason for
my vigil—comes up the road. My jailor. A girl.
Barely in double figures. Tall for her years. Thin
and drawn out. Carrying not one bag over her
shoulder but two. What can this mean?

As she approaches the gate she hurriedly ties one bag to the post and then continues onwards, up the hollow road. Perplexed, I stay where I am and wait. A short while later a cry drifts down the hollow. Long, low, guttural. The hills resound with it. Something in great pain and torment.

The sound of it is overwhelming. It pins me to the spot and I am utterly prone. The hollow suddenly feels open and exposed. A crushing sensation envelopes my chest, threatening to split my ribcage along the sternum. I press myself against the crumbling stonework. I try to breathe. My heart in my throat, cheeks wet with tears. Goodness and mercy. Comfort me, comfort me.

No further sounds. A brittle quiet descends on the hollow. After what seems like an age the girl returns, coming back down the road in a half walk, half lumbering run. As she passes she stops and looks up, straight in my direction. Does she see me? I try not to even blink. After a few, achingly long seconds she resumes her path, down the hollow road and out of sight.

+

Valley of the shadow. All is quiet, but the memory of that primal cry still makes me wretched with fear. What could make such a sound? You'll get you what you need, she said. I have longed for an end to the silence, but no, not that. It is out there somewhere. Are you come here to die? She said that too. I keep the axe near. For thou art with me.

+

But before the fear consumes you, think on this. A mere child, barely in double figures, may freely walk up and down the hollow road. Apparently unharmed. Whatever it is, it must be caged. Remember that.

+

I try to decide if I am a believer in fate. There are no accidents. I have said so before. Touch the horseshoes. Cross yourself. Call on Him if you must. The old prayers, unsaid for decades. Dry on the tongue.

+

And yes. I must confess that I have prayed. Prayed for life or death. An end to the waiting. To the havoc of fear. The vaulting panic. But I am sure that His mercy has never been here. His jurisdiction, such that it is, ends at the line of crags and hills that lean in around me. I am lost in a place of darkness. A place over which something altogether older presides. Any prayers answered are done so by an incalculably different authority, and my debt is yet to be settled. My past self would feel foolish even thinking such things, much less saying them, but there it is.

+

More words stir in the murk waters. *He maketh me to lie down in green pastures.*

Backwaters of the memory. Silted rivers. Stagnant marshes.

But they are rote words. You realise this? Meaningless. If words are to work you must make them yourself. Conjure them out of the very earth.

+

Be still. Bed down there a while. You're safe. Surely. Out of sight. You'll get you what you need.

+

Among the usual provisions, the bag contains matches, ethanol and gauze. A prayer answered. I am no doctor but the wound looks inflamed. I rub it with some of the ethanol and apply a fresh dressing. The pain is excruciating. If I can get the spirit stove to work this will be my first hot meal.

+

A corked jar of chicken stock, onions, potatoes, carrots, eggs, oatmeal. With some initial resistance the stove finally fires up. After countless days of cold it is something miraculous. I make soup with some of the stock and vegetables, warming my hands for the first time while it is cooking. In the morning I will make an oatmeal gruel. Delirious.

+

Strength begins to seep back into my body. The chanting of the stream recedes. The wound aches afresh but it is a necessary pain. Those persistent thoughts, those anxieties, voices, they seem to diminish. It is good to have a body. To feel.

+

Night returns. Sleep is a tide. Endlessly retreating. Drifting towards the horizon. And I am stranded. And there again, you. I feel you. You are always here now. A strange comfort, even though my heart races.

+

The hills lean in, apply their poultice. I am being drawn out. In the open I am prone, but I wander nonetheless. I stay close to the shieling at first. Testing the ground. But soon enough I know where I must go. I have not heard that cry again, but the thought of it sickens me. It is out there. Up the hollow road. Caged. But despite the fear there is something else. Something close to pity. My heart trembles at the thought.

+

The trap quivers. Tension in the spring. It will bite soon enough. And then I am lost. I look once more at the map. Swirling patterns. All those lines. And my name. Right at the heart.

+

After days of aimless wandering it comes to this. Shortly after dawn I take the hollow road north. A moderate climb, but the wound hurts and I have to rest several times. Once I swear I hear footsteps behind me, and I turn quickly, but there is nothing except the sound of my own pulse, hammering in my ears.

After about a quarter of a mile the road passes through a collection of ruined buildings. One is a farmhouse. Its whitewash is peeling and dirty, its windows boarded up. A derelict barn faces it on the other side of the road, across an expanse of courtyard. Adjoining the barn is a maze of pens, traps and folds, interconnected by a series of gates, most of which are rotten and broken. At its centre there seems to be an older structure made from drystone wall which has been further embellished, probably over subsequent generations, by wood, wire and corrugated metal, creating a series of passageways and enclosures. The stonework core is relatively intact, but the newer materials show signs of prolonged weathering and decay. The effect is disquieting. I can think of nothing else but that distorted wire lattice and its avian attendant, dwelling in perpetual shade.

In the mud that covers most of the courtyard I can see fresh prints. The girl? A prickly thrill of unease begins to unfurl around me, and I wish that I had brought a knife. Or better still, the axe.

Above the centre door is an enormous pair of animal horns. Beneath them a large caulked horseshoe. Scattered in the dirt below the door are clumps of moss, and on closer inspection parts of the door itself are daubed with a white, greasy substance. It smells foul.

Look away. It was a mistake to come here. As I make to leave I distinctly hear movement from within the barn. I stand rigidly still and listen. Nothing but the panicked motions of my own body, which seem to cloud the air around my head. I hold my breath and wait. Still nothing. I edge backwards, scanning the ground.

Suddenly, the sound of something metal falling hard and being dragged across a stone floor. And then the door shuddering as a massive weight is thrown against it. Again and again. I stand transfixed.

And then that *other* sound. Coming through the door. A sound I have heard once before, across a quarter-mile of field and meadow. But hearing it here, in such proximity, is a different matter. It tears me out of my stupor. I know it means just one thing. Every cell in my body screams it. Are you come here to die? Goodness and mercy.

I turn and run as the door shakes again. It will not last another impact. The wound flares in agony and I know that—if pursued—I will never make it back to the shieling. I scan left and right, looking for a means of escape. Fifty or so yards down the track I see a field-gate on the right, partially obscured by small trees. I focus on the pain because pain means life. As the gate looms before me I throw myself at it, attempting to clear it. My lower body grazes it clumsily, and I twist, landing on my back, winded. Dragging myself into the ditch below the drystone wall, I press my face into the cool grass, trembling, heart pounding, the taste of vomit in my mouth.

I am still. I am safe. I am out of sight. I am—

+

II

I wake to find myself lying face down in the
ditch. There are words in my mouth but I do not
know them. The taste of dirt and grasses. Bite
your tongue.

For a long time I listen but there are no sounds.
Dead quiet. I rise carefully, expecting a sharp jolt
of pain, but there is nothing. I scan the top of
the drystone wall. Up and down the hollow road.
Nothing. Alone. I sink back down and wait with
my back to the wall, clutching handfuls of grass.
Shaking.

Dusk is approaching. It will be night soon. I
cannot risk going back along the hollow road.
It is too exposed. I look up through the field to
the horizon, following the contours of the walls,
looking for some means of passage.

Suddenly, along the length of the nearest wall
I see movement. Something small and grey,
coming out of the stone itself. And then gone.

Follow. Quick. Keeping my eye on where the
thing vanished I scramble along the lower edge
of the field. There. A gap in the wall. Invisible
from my previous position. I follow the lower
wall as it rises up to meet it. Stay down. Out of
sight.

And in the next field, there, again. Grey.
Motionless. Crouched down. Ears flattened

across her back. Large, dark eyes. A hare. She takes up. As if the thought—the name alone—had startled her. Through the tall grasses. At speed. Follow the needle. I track her light imprint as it zig-zags across the field. You'll get you what you need.

We continue our game, on through the next field, and the next. Each time she crouches down until I get near. And then bolts. Erratic. Wild. Follow me.

Moments later, on the horizon, a familiar outline. The ash-tree that shelters the byre. Home. Safe in the middle of hills.
Thank you, thank you.

+

The old prayers. Dry on the tongue. You must conjure something out of the very earth.

Where are you now, my guide? I can almost hear the rattle of your heart—*be quick, be safe, be quick, be safe*—

+

I light a candle and sit in the gloom, watching shadows flutter across the whitewashed walls. My hands summon the silhouettes of animals from the flame. Among them, hare, fox, raven. I welcome them like family.

+

The shieling, quiet. Almost peaceful. When did the clock stop its ticking?

+

Night comes. Vagrant thoughts. Drawn back up the hollow road. Like fingers to a wound. Animal horns. A caulked horseshoe. Clumps of moss. The door, daubed in grease. And *that* sound.

+

Grip the axe in the darkness. Feel its dull blade against your skin. Whisper to it as the candle flickers out.

+

Give it back, something whispers in the fever of half-sleep. *Give it back.*

+

And in the black of night the stream. Chanting. Something approaching words.

+

In the dim morning the silhouette of a large bird crests the brow of the cragged hill that faces the shieling. But it swiftly turns, and, wheeling, returns to whence it came.

Later, chafing rain. The sound of it on the slate shieling roof. And on the tin byre roof. A two-part melody of attrition. I listen with something approaching rapture.

When the rain has done, everything glistens. A new skin, after the sloughing of the old. I stand in the doorway to get the scent of it. White foaming water out on the hills. Desperate to be anywhere other than here. New channels, pooling in the lower meadows.

And something else. The hills, stones and bracken. And from them, an animal shape. Broken loose.

+

The form of a fox, but drained of colour, and larger—much larger—than any I have ever seen. Goodness and mercy. That fluttering in my throat—

+

And then gone. Back to the grey earth.

+

Days later I see it again. Stalking in the dusk.
Patrolling a phalanx of outlying trees beyond
the narrow wood, lower down the hollow.
Slow movements, circling. Clearly the mark
of something.

+

But the mark of what? Instantly, I think of the
hare. I think of her out there. A small form
lost within the vast dark. Crouched down.
Motionless. Silent, but for the rattle of her
heart. And always behind her. On her trail.
This predator.

+

A pang of sympathy. I too have felt it. Dogged. Have hidden. Have watched the night. You with the dark eyes. Innocent one. What do you see beneath it all?

+

I imagine their game of chase. Among the oldest in all creation. Each compelled to play their part. A trick of heredity.

+

I watch the hills for what seems like days. No sign of one or the other. I eat next to nothing and take only a little water. I begin to feel stretched out. My skin, almost translucent. This cannot continue.

+

My guide. Come to me. *Please*.

+

Once I catch the form of a large, black bird, wheeling, piercing the clouds. But it is lost all too quickly.

+

And then mist. A return to the old ways. The hollow, wreathed in grey. Dense. Close. Thick against the shieling's window. Time, measureless since the clock ceased its ticking, seems to lose its way entirely. But at least there is one comforting thought—surely she is safe out there, clothed in grey? Out of sight.

+

And what of myself? I find now that I have given up any pretence of eating. My bodily functions seem to be shutting down. Perhaps I will simply root here and wither to nothingness. I am lost. The past blurs.

But there is something I need to say. Something unspeakable. I try to remember. I—

+

Days in which the only certainties are these.
The shapes of this room. Its surfaces and edges.
Whitewashed walls. The world outside the
shieling, increasingly unreal. A winding sheet of
grey. Have I not been here always?

+

Perhaps I am a delusion of these dreaming hills?
How did you get here, wretched creature?
I cannot tell. A bird with a broken wing.
Unable to fly.

+

Eventually, storm. It had been coming for days.
Even my dull senses could apprehend it. Far off,
rumbling. The whole hollow seeming to rejoice
in its mutterings.

It was presaged in the early hours of day by the
barking of a raven. Circling. Somewhere high
up. Up above the shieling. Was this the bird I
had glimpsed in the previous days?

Lying in the gloom of the not-quite-morning
I felt myself no longer tied to the land. Felt my
tongue and glottis dance in new combinations.
Felt the cloying, heavy air. The sudden updraft.
The thrill of an eddy. The whole canopy of day
hatching. About to burst forth.

And from that height I saw encroaching banks
of black cloud coming from the west. To the
east a grey, milky brightness, pierced by the first
glimmers of light. The veiled topography of the
hollow swam beneath us. Jutting skerries of rock,
blue-black, glistening, rose and then fell, queasy,
seasick. There would be thunder.

With the first tremors of it the bird barked and
veered. Plummeting. Straight and hard. The
feeling was vertiginous. Thrilling. Ecstatic. But
I could not hold the line, and I fell. My perch
in the sky lost. I returned to my body, shaking,
trembling.

The tremors lasted well into the night. The shieling, the fields, the hills, all of us, convulsing. The sky's great vessel, crashing, crashing.

+

And now I crouch by the window to watch the last of the engine's copper-coloured fire. See, in brief flashes, that ageless face, looking back out of the mass of stone and earth, across the hollow. A face of many eyes. Are you come here to die? Surely.

And all the while, below the storm's violence, below crescendo and decrescendo, the chanting of the stream. Stirred to a frenzy. A primal music. Elemental.

I add my voice to the polyphony. Shouting, screaming.

+

Dream. The passing of ages. I see the hollow become a lake. Then I see it drowned. Sunk to the bottom of an ocean. Everything dead. Everything written anew.

+

I awake to a sallow dawn and think of the thrush of the hollow wood. Will a bird ever sing again?

+

The day passes in perfect stillness and silence. There are miniature lakes in the fields and the hollow road shines like silver. I walk out to survey the devastation. The ash-tree that presided over the byre has fallen. Its largest limb puncturing the roof before demolishing the building entirely. A desecration. I wonder about that coil of metal. Perhaps its twisted shape foretold its own destruction? Whatever it was, it now lies buried beneath wood, stone and metal. Out of sight.

I sit in the cluster of ruinous stone watching the day edge blindly towards night. The sound of water becomes slowly audible. A low, droning note. And darkness begins to seep into the shieling, pooling along its edges.

Later, another sound. Somewhere lower down the hollow. Faint. High pitched. Keening. As the dark thickens it intensifies. An awful sense of foreboding.

I close my eyes.

+

I see the boy, sitting on the doorstep of a terraced house. The street, the sky, empty. Din of traffic in the distance. Inside the house, the father's body is laid out in an open coffin. Hands crossed in repose. Hands calloused from decades of manual labour. Now at rest.

The door opens. Won't you come in? the mother asks. It will be dark soon.

He tries to speak, but the words lodge in his throat. How can he tell her what he has seen? That during the night's vigil, in the trembling darkness, there was a darker figure standing over the body. That even now he is here, in the fading light, standing at the door's threshold. Eyes the palest of blues.

The keening sound intensifies as the figure
loosens itself from the shadows. Advances
towards the bed. My heart.

A contorted human shape leans over me.
Pale blue eyes, regarding me intently.

You must come, he says at last without words.
And into my hand he places a shimmering, red
thread. It writhes in my palm like something
living. And when I look up he is gone.

+

The thread is sinewy, mucilage covered, foul smelling. It stretches out through the open doorway and trails off across the field and down the hollow, glimmering in the darkness. I can do nothing but follow.

+

I cross the hollow road and continue through field after sodden field, soon ankle-deep in mud. I come to a swollen brook and fall to my hands and knees. In the moonlight I can see the forms of drowned plants, trembling below the water's surface.

I cross the brook and press onwards. As I approach a wall that borders the far side of the next field the sound becomes clearer. A cry. A newborn's high pitched, mewling cry. I run.

The thread worms through a small passageway built into the wall's foundations. It is much too small for me to pass through, and so I climb, the stones tumbling. On the other side a shallow pit. And in it, the source of the cry.

+

She is coiled in agony. Her lower body caught in a wire snare, which, as she struggles, bites deeper into her flesh, innards exposed, the bright source of the shimmering thread.

+

On seeing me, the wretched creature redoubles her efforts to be free of the trap. Cries of pain. I reach down to touch her, stroking her matted fur. Murmuring soft words of comfort.

+

And as I lean over her she stills and looks at me, sidelong, unblinking, her large, dark eye filled with bright pain and fear.

Kill me, she says without words. *Kill me quickly.*

I cannot. My words ring out in the damp night air. Empty. Hollow.

You must kill me.

I place my hands on her again. Her wildness like a torrent, her heartbeat racing, speeding towards her life's end.

I cannot.

The pain is unbearable. Please.

I gently release the snare and lift the hare's head in my hands, feeling the delicate bones of her neck. Life and death, held in balance.

I cannot—

+

Suddenly I catch the shape of something moving, in the periphery of my vision.

I look up. And—

+

Do it. Do it now.
That fluttering in my throat.
Please.
I can barely breathe.
Please.

+

The shape slowly steps out of the shadows.
Taking on moonlit form. A fox. But larger.
Much larger.

I see the great wound on its flank. The chain
about its neck. *Broken loose*. It bares its teeth.

And in those brief sickening moments I see
myself as I am seen. Predator and prey. The game
of chase. Among the oldest in all creation.

In the sky overhead I hear the raven. Feel the air
move from its circling closeness.

Are you come here to die?

+

I am running, running. Across the field. Over the brook. Not looking back. The night thick with the hare's cries. Goodness and mercy. The old prayers. Where are you?

+

Her cries fill the darkness long into the night.
Each an agony of shame. How could I leave her
with those scavengers?

I crouch, back against the door, gripping the axe.
Longing for silence. An end to it all.

+

In the pale early light her cries finally fall below the threshold of hearing, and I fall into a fitful, dreamless sleep.

+

Some hours later I awake. How many I cannot say. How can morning rise out of such a night? It is something sickening.

Immediately I think of the hare, and my complicity in her torture. Why had I not the courage? It was almost too much to bear. More than that—the thought of the fox and raven, picking over her carcass—

+

Picking up the axe I open the door and cross the threshold. There is a sweet yet acrid smell in the air. I turn and see that the door is smeared with a white, greasy substance. And on the ground a scattering of fresh moss.

+

Outside in the hollow there is a pathway through the drowned fields. I follow. But when I come to the wall with its narrow passageway there is no kill site. No traces of blood or fur. No scent of death. Nothing but the snare, primed and hidden. Waiting. I rip it out and retrace my steps through the hollow and back to the shieling.

+

Throughout the day I survey the hills and meadows. Everything empty. No movement, not even a breeze.

+

But in the evening it returns. That high pitched, mewling cry. Faint. Disarticulate. Growing more insistent with the dimming of the light. My hairs standing on end.

+

How can this be? I had torn out the snare. How was she still alive, and how caught again? I stand in the window. Somewhere, high up, I know, the raven is circling, waiting. I can almost hear the beating of its wings. And out there in the gloom of the wood, a fox's eyes, watching.

+

I light a candle and sit. Hunched in the corner. Readying myself.

+

You know why I am here, he says, wordlessly, from the doorway. Pale blue eyes, regarding me intently.
I don't want this, I cry.
He moves silently towards me, his twisted crown glimmering in the candlelight.
But you have chosen it.
I don't understand.
The candle flickers violently, as if caught in a sudden draught.
You called her and now you are bound together.
His shadow, dancing across the wall—no longer something human.
You know what you must do.
The shimmering, red thread writhes in my palm.
I cannot.
But he is gone.

+

Valley of the shadow. The longest night. I pray
for the agony of the wound to return. Something
like life. Give me pain, I will take it, that it
will remove hers. I will suffer for her. I strike
myself. Throw myself against the shieling's walls.
Nothing. I am senseless.

+

Again her cries continue well into the night. And as the darkness reaches its fullness another cry joins her's in awful union. Long, low, guttural. And above the shieling, circling, the raven begins its barking.

+

The sounds trail off as the first glimmers of day break across the hollow.

I have never been more thankful for daylight.
I will close my eyes.

+

I see fields and meadows. An old, winding country lane. Low hills hazed in the distance. A family, walking. The boy trails slightly behind the others.

At a bend in the lane his eye is caught by something in the hedgerow. A bird's nest, with the mother crouched down, brooding. She returns his gaze, sidelong, unblinking. Her large, dark eye bright with fear. Just one, the boy sings to her, gently, just this once.

It is done in a moment, the egg still warm in his hand. So warm and delicate. The palest of blues. But when he looks back down the lane the others are gone. He cries out but there is no answer. The sun, only a moment earlier high in the sky, is now beginning to set, a blue pall descending over the fields.

He looks to the horizon and there he finds them. Silhouettes, faint and impossibly small, but it is them. Two larger and one smaller, trailing slightly behind the others. He sees the lane stretch out between them, seemingly infinite, tortuous. He watches them. Slowly slipping from sight.

Some hours later I awake. How many I cannot say. I am lying in the shieling's wide open doorway.

The light is already failing. It will not be long.

+

I rise and stand by the window, looking out across the grey-black fields. Although I cannot see them, I know they are out there. Hare. Fox. Raven. Each waiting to play their part. And so the awful chorus begins.

+

Do you not see it? he says, advancing from the doorway.
I don't understand.
They have come for you. There is no escape.
He places a hand on my shoulder.
You must prepare yourself.

+

The realisation stuns me. *Prepare yourself.*

I had come here to escape my past, or so I had thought. Hiding from unknown pursuers. From retribution—I had done something unspeakable, I was sure of it.

And *they* had come.

An answer from the very land itself. Lines on the map, connecting us, bringing us together.

The keening sound intensifies.

+

You know what you must do.

+

A mercy killing. A death of kindness. A rest that is the gift of innocence.

+

Courage. I see it now. In the end everything yields. There is no other way.

+

In a rocky hollow you will find her. Follow the needle. Its shimmering thread.

I hold her head in my hands.

Do it swiftly, she says without words. She looks at me, sidelong, her large, dark eye, filled with bright pain and fear. Goodness and mercy. *Look away, if you're scared.*

+

I bury her deeply. So deep the axe hits bedrock.
I will not let the fox or raven find her.

+

Some hours later I awake. How many I cannot say. I am lying in the shieling's wide open doorway.

There are words in my mouth but I do not know them. I rise and stand, looking out across the hollow.

+

I had buried her. But she is here, waiting. On the rough track that winds its way up from the field-gate. My heart. I cannot feel my heart.

+

I remember now. It all comes back to me. Flooding. Here's all I have. The sum total of a life. *Give it back.* I leave it at the shieling's door. A mark to go with all the others. Safe in the middle of hills.

+

I am ready. She rises and turns. Looks at me, over her shoulder. Waiting. I follow her and we walk together.

+

Each step is an unmooring. Habitually, I turn and look back at the shieling.

They have come.

They must have been close by. Circling. The fox paws at the slumped form in the shieling's doorway. Still, lifeless. The raven barks from its perch on the slate roof. Ruffling its feathers, as if shaking off rainwater. Look away.

+

We walk north up the hollow road. I am by her side. As we pass the farm my eye is caught by the barn door, which, broken, swings open on its hinges. It is only a moment, but when I look back up the hollow road she is gone.

I cry out but there is no answer. The sun, only a moment earlier high in the sky, is now beginning to set, a blue pall descending over the hollow.

I look to the horizon and there I find her. A silhouette, faint and impossibly small, but it is her. Crouched down, ears flattened across her back. I see the road stretch out between us, seemingly infinite, tortuous. I watch her.

She looks at me, over her shoulder. Waiting.

Follow me.

By the same author

· Landings (2009)
· Field Notes, Volume One (2012)*
· Moor Glisk (2012)
· Limnology (2012)
· Memorious Earth (2015)*
· Beyond the Fell Wall (2015)
· The Pale Ladder (2016)

with Autumn Richardson

Printed in March 2023
by Rotomail Italia S.p.A., Vignate (MI) - Italy